PINKY BLOOM

AND THE

CASE OF THE

MAGICAL MENORAH

JUDY PRESS

ILLUSTRATED BY
ERICA-JANE WATERS

KAR-BEN
PUBLISHING

KAR-BEN PUBLISHING®
An imprint of Lerner Publishing Group, Inc.
241 First Avenue North
Minneapolis, MN 55401 USA

Website address: www.karben.com

Main body text set in Bembo Std regular.
Typeface provided by Monotype Typography.

Library of Congress Cataloging-in-Publication Data

Names: Press, Judy, 1944– author. | Waters, Erica-Jane, illustrator.
Title: Pinky Bloom and the case of the magical menorah / by Judy Press ;
    illustrated by Erica-Jane Waters.
Description: Case of the magical menorah | Series: Pinky Bloom | Audience:
    Ages 8–12. | Audience: Grades 4–6. | Summary: Brooklyn's greatest detective
    Penina "Pinky" Bloom and her brother Avi solve the case of the mysterious
    menorah when an ancient Israeli coin is stolen from her family's synagogue.
Identifiers: LCCN 2020003372 | ISBN 9781541576254 | ISBN 9781541576261
    (paperback)
Subjects: CYAC: Mystery and detective stories. | Stealing—Fiction. | Forgery—
    Fiction. | Jews—United States—Fiction.
Classification: LCC PZ7.P921927 Pg 2021 | DDC [Fic]—dc23

LC record available at https://lccn.loc.gov/2020003372

Manufactured in the United States of America
1-46605-47608-1/20/2021

For Allan J. Press, my one and only
—J.P.

Chapter One

I'm Penina "Pinky" Bloom, Brooklyn's greatest kid detective and sister to Avi, the world's most annoying little brother.

A pair of my favorite sunglasses was missing, and he was the prime suspect!

Taped to his door was a sign that said, *KEEP OUT! SECRET AGENT IN TRAINING!*

Yesterday, Avi had wanted to be a shark hunter. The day before that, it was a race car driver. It looked like he'd already changed his mind again.

"Open up, Avi!" I shouted. "It's time for dinner."

The door opened a crack, and he stuck out his head. "I'm busy being a secret agent, Pinky. What do you want?"

Avi was wearing a floppy hat, a long black rain-coat, and MY SUNGLASSES!

"I want those back—now," I demanded.

"But I need them, Pinky. Secret agents wear sunglasses so they don't get recognized."

Before I could tell Avi that he's a second-grader, *not* a secret agent, the doorbell rang.

I figured it might be my best friend, Lucy Chang. She lives two floors below me, and we'd invited her over for dinner. Tonight was the 25th day of Kislev, the first night of Hanukkah.

Dad didn't look up from his computer as I raced past him to get to the door.

"Who is it?" I asked, standing on tiptoes and squinting through the peephole.

"It's me, Mrs. Glick, from next door," a faint voice answered.

I slipped off the chain and opened the door.

"Sorry to bother you, Pinky," she said. "Is your mom or dad home?"

Mrs. Glick is really old. She wears thick glasses because she can't see too well. One time, when I had a sore throat, she brought me a bowl of chicken soup, and the chicken's feet were still inside. Gross!

"Come in, Mrs. Glick," Dad said. "So nice to see you. I'll call my wife."

Grown-ups usually talk about boring stuff, but just in case, I hung around. My cat, D. J., was sitting by the bookcase, so I crouched down to pet him.

"Please sit down, Mrs. Glick," Mom said, shoving aside a pair of dirty gym socks that Avi had left on the couch. "How can we help you?"

Mrs. Glick began her story. "You've met my son, Buzzy," she said. "He's a very big archaeologist. He works in Israel, digging for ancient artifacts."

This must've sounded boring to D. J., because he wandered off. But I stayed where I was, picking at the scab I'd gotten when I skinned my knee playing soccer.

Ancient artifacts could be cool. I once found a penny from 1974 on the sidewalk outside my building. My dad said it wasn't old enough to be worth more than one cent, but I kept it for good luck.

Mrs. Glick continued, "After his last trip to Israel, Buzzy brought home a menorah. He said I must always keep it with me. But today I leave to visit my sister in Florida. I can't take it on the plane, and I don't want to leave it behind in my empty apartment. What if someone breaks in? Or what if there's a fire?"

"We'll be happy to keep it safe while you're away," Mom quickly offered. I could tell she didn't think any break-ins or fires would happen, but good neighbors do each other favors.

"Wonderful!" Mrs. Glick said. "I'll bring it over right now. You can even light it for Hanukkah if you want. But first, you should know . . ." She lowered her voice. "My Buzzy told me it's not like any other menorah. This one is magical!"

I quit picking at my scab. Hanukkah had just gotten a whole lot more interesting!

Chapter Two

Mrs. Glick brought over her magical menorah and left it on the dining room table.

In kindergarten, I made a menorah out of cardboard and Popsicle sticks. My mom thought it was awesome. That's a mom thing.

The Glicks' menorah was much fancier than that. It had nine branches, one for each of the eight days of Hanukkah, plus the *shamash*, or helper candle, to light the others. On the top of each branch was a silver candleholder that held the candles.

It was almost dinnertime. Avi was supposed to

help me set the table, but he was nowhere in sight.

I knocked on his door, and when he didn't answer, I yelled, "If you don't come out right now, you're going to miss dinner!"

Avi never misses a meal. He bolted out of his room and raced down the hallway. "Hey, what's this?" he asked when he saw the menorah.

I explained that we were keeping it until Mrs. Glick got home. "And she told us it's magical," I added.

"Wow! That means I can make a wish and get anything I want," Avi said.

"Not so fast. Just because someone says something doesn't mean it's true."

"But maybe the menorah *is* magical!"

"Okay, let's test it. Ask the menorah to fly across the living room."

"It can't do stuff like that! A menorah doesn't have wings."

"Okay, so ask it a question, and we'll see if it knows the answer."

Avi addressed the menorah. "Will Grandma Phyllis visit us for Hanukkah?"

Suddenly, a deep voice roared, "Your wish is my command, but only if you clean up your room."

Avi and I stared at each other with our mouths open. What was going on? Had the magical menorah really spoken?

Dad crawled out from under the dining room table. "Got you!" he said, laughing. "I had you going for a second, didn't I?"

Grown-ups always think they're funny, but they're not.

Just then, the doorbell rang. Maybe it was Lucy!

"Guess who, darlings?" a familiar voice sang out. "It's me, Grandma Phyllis!"

"I told you so, Pinky!" Avi said. "I knew the menorah was magical."

Here's the thing: Grandma Phyllis *always* comes for Hanukkah!

But it *was* kind of weird that she showed up right after Avi asked the magical menorah if she was coming.

"How was the trip to Brooklyn?" Dad asked as he opened the door. Grandma Phyllis lives far away, in Queens, so it can take her forever to get to our apartment.

"It was fine!" she said. "I took that car-sharing ride. I had a very nice driver who told me all about his visit to Israel." She stepped inside and set her suitcase down.

That's when I remembered that whenever Grandma Phyllis comes for a visit, she stays in Avi's room, and he moves into mine.

Ugh, Hanukkah might not be so fun after all!

Chapter Three

Every year on the first night of Hanukkah, Dad tells us the story of Great-Great-Grandma Bloom's menorah.

"Her family had to leave their home in a rush. They could only take a few things with them on their long journey. Now, what do you think they wouldn't leave behind?"

"The menorah!" Avi and I chimed, like every time we heard the story.

Dad nodded and continued, "On Hanukkah, we light Great-Great-Grandma Bloom's menorah and remember her. We're also reminded of the brave Judah Maccabee and the rededication of the Temple after its desecration."

Avi pointed to the Glicks' menorah. "Maybe the magical menorah is really, really old and belonged to Judah Maccabee!"

"The Maccabees rededicated the Temple in 165 BCE," I reminded him. "There's no way it's *that* menorah."

"Let's light it tonight," Avi said.

Dad agreed. "But for the rest of the holiday, we'll light our family's menorah."

Mom walked into the living room. "Pinky, I just got a text from Lucy's mother," she said. "Her grandmother isn't feeling well, and Lucy can't come over tonight."

I felt bad about Lucy's grandmother, and I hoped I would still see Lucy tomorrow night. She was supposed to come with us to our synagogue's Hanukkah party. In the early spring, I always go with her family to the Lunar New Year parade in Chinatown.

"Pinky, I need you and Avi to help make the latkes," Grandma Phyllis called out.

After I peeled the potatoes, Avi grated them. Then Mom and Grandma Phyllis fried the latkes in oil.

Next, we gathered around the Glicks' menorah. Dad lit the shamash first, and together we recited the blessings.

Barukh atah Adonai, Eloheinu, melekh ha'olam asher kidishanu b'mitz'votav v'tzivanu l'had'lik neir shel Chanukah. (Amein.)

Barukh atah Adonai, Eloheinu, melekh ha'olam she'asah nisim la'avoteinu bayamim haheim baziman hazeh. (Amein.)

Barukh atah Adonai, Eloheinu, melekh ha'olam shehecheyanu v'kiyimanu v'higi'anu laz'man hazeh. (Amein.)

"Time to eat!" Mom announced.

Avi stabbed his fork into a latke. "I can eat a hundred of these!" he bragged.

After dinner, Grandma Phyllis suggested we sing a Hanukkah song. We had just started to sing "I Had a Little Dreidel" when all of a sudden, the lights in our apartment went out, and it was pitch black!

Chapter Four

A few seconds later, the lights flickered and came back on. "If it happens again, I'll call Mr. Norman," Mom said. "Who wants dessert?"

Mr. Norman is the superintendent for our building. Everyone calls him the super. His job is to keep the building in good shape and fix problems. Supers get called to fix *lots* of problems, like the time I was little and tried to flush a toy down the toilet. Or when Avi stopped up the sink and flooded the downstairs apartment.

Right now, Avi was getting impatient. "Can I

open my presents?" he whined.

Some kids get a gift each night of Hanukkah, but in my family, we open all our gifts on the first night.

Grandma Phyllis brought out two large boxes covered in Hanukkah wrapping paper. "This is for Avi," she said, handing him his gift. "And this one is for Pinky."

Avi tore into his box. "A spy kit!" he yelled. "And it's got binoculars, night vision goggles, a fingerprinting set, and a flashlight."

Great, I thought. *Maybe I'll get my sunglasses back!*

I carefully unwrapped my gift. "A digital camera! Thank you. It's perfect for a detective."

My old camera used to belong to Grandpa Bloom. It took great pictures, but I wasn't able to upload them to the computer.

I also got a set of watercolor paints and a book about a famous Jewish French Impressionist painter, Camille Pissarro. One time, my class went to the National Gallery of Art in Washington, DC, where we saw some of his paintings. Maybe one day my artwork will hang in a museum!

Mom and Dad and Grandma Phyllis unwrapped their gifts too. Then Mom said, "It's getting late. Pinky and Avi, please clean up and put away your gifts."

We helped the adults carry all the dinner dishes into the kitchen. Then Avi went to get ready for bed.

"Don't bring all your stuff into my room," I warned. I followed him out of the kitchen, through the living room, and all the way to his bedroom door.

"I'm just bringing my catcher's mitt, my basketball shoes, my Yankees blanket, my stuffed dinosaur, and my spy kit."

"You'd better not be planning to spy on me, Avi Bloom! If you do, I'm telling Mom."

When I got back to the living room, I gasped. Every single candle on the Glicks' menorah was out. Usually, candles on a menorah burn down at different speeds and go out one at a time. I looked more closely and saw that most of the candles had plenty of wax left, so they should still be burning.

I got goose bumps, thinking about the strange things that had been happening ever since we got this magical menorah!

Chapter Five

The next night, Lucy came over. "How's your grandmother?" I asked her.

"Much better!" she said, tossing her coat on my bed. "She said I should go to the party and have a good time. I'm glad I'm not going to miss it! Last year was so much fun."

She was right about the synagogue Hanukkah party being fun. Everyone got to spin dreidels and eat delicious food. This year, Avi's friend Max was going to perform a magic act.

I told Lucy about the strange things that were

happening. "First, Grandma Phyllis showed up, then our lights went out, and after that the candles on the menorah blew out all at once."

"Those could all just be coincidences," Lucy said. "Wait and see if anything else happens."

Avi barged into my room. "I'm going undercover to the Hanukkah party," he announced. "Do you think anyone will recognize me?"

He was wearing his spy uniform. The night vision goggles and the flashlight from his new spy kit were sticking out of the pockets of his raincoat.

Lucy put her hand over her mouth to keep from laughing. I rolled my eyes. "Avi, I told you to give me those sunglasses back."

Just then, my dad stuck his head in the doorway. "Let's go, kids. We don't want to miss out on the fun."

At the synagogue, the social hall was decorated for Hanukkah. Blue and white streamers hung from the ceiling, and each table had a candy dish filled with chocolate *gelt*.

"Over here, Pinky!" I heard someone shout.

It was Shira Newman. She's in my class, and her brother, Max, is Avi's best friend.

"You should sit with us," Shira said. "The party's going to be awesome. Max is the entertainment.

He's been practicing his magic act for days."

Shira's dad is president of the synagogue. After everyone was seated, he walked to the front of the room and lit the menorah while we said the prayer together.

"Thank you for coming to our annual Hanukkah party," Mr. Newman said. "Tonight, I'd like to extend a special thank-you to Mrs. Glick for her donation of an ancient Israeli coin. Eventually, we hope to sell this coin to a collector. We'll use the money to make improvements to the synagogue and help our community members. But for now, we'd like all of you to enjoy this historic object."

The audience applauded loudly.

"Folks, the coin is on display in the lobby," Mr. Newman added. "Stop by and take a look. Now, enjoy your evening, and have a happy Hanukkah!"

A bunch of people closer to the front of the room lined up by the buffet table. It was going to be a while before it was our turn to eat. Shira turned to Lucy, Avi, and me. "Come on. I'll show you the coin before we get in line for food."

"Don't be long," Mom told us.

I told her she didn't need to worry. "Avi would never let us miss dinner!"

In the lobby, Shira led us over to a small podium with a glass display case. We crowded around it with a few of the other party guests. Inside the case, the coin was propped up so that we could see both sides.

The coin wasn't much bigger than a dime. On the front side was an image of a goblet surrounded by ancient Hebrew letters, and on the back was a carving of three stems of a plant.

A letter typed on fancy paper said that the coin was from the time of the first revolt in Jerusalem.

I pulled out my new camera and took a picture of the coin to show to my teacher when I went back to school. Then we headed back to our table in the social hall.

We were about to get dinner when my mom asked, "Where's Avi?"

That's when I realized he wasn't with us any-more. "I'll go look for him," I volunteered. "He must still be out in the lobby."

I headed back to the lobby, which was empty now.

"Pssst! Pinky, I'm over here. It's me!"

I looked where the voice was coming from and saw Avi peeking out from behind a fake plant.

"What are you doing out here, Avi? You're going to miss dinner!"

"Shhhh! Keep it down, Pinky. I don't want anyone to know it's me."

"You have to come back to the social hall," I
said. "Mom and Dad were worried when they didn't
know where you were."

"This is my job, Pinky! Listen—"

I had heard enough. I grabbed Avi by his shirt
collar and pulled him out from behind the plant.

Every once in a while, a big sister has to get tough
with her little brother!

Chapter Six

Back at our table, Avi kept trying to get my attention. He tugged on my sleeve and said, "Pinky, I have to tell you something . . ."

Dad cut him off. "You'll tell her later," he said. "Let's go eat."

We walked to the buffet table and piled chicken, broccoli, and latkes onto our plates. Then Shira said, "Let's get dessert too. I saw they have *sufganiyot* and other kinds of donuts."

I explained to Lucy why we eat fried foods at Hanukkah. "In ancient times, there was only enough oil in the Temple to last one day. It was a miracle that it lasted for eight."

We were headed to the dessert table when someone said, "Is that you, Pinky? I'm over here, darling."

It was Madame Olga, a part-time babysitter and full-time psychic who helps out when I'm on a case.

"So when are you and Avi coming to visit me?" she asked. "You don't have to wait for a mystery."

"We're on winter break, so we can visit you this week," I said.

"Perfect! I'll be at the Newmans' house tomorrow while Mr. and Mrs. Newman are at work. You should come over. Now, go eat your dinner before it gets cold."

I said goodbye to Madame Olga and hurried back to our table. As soon as I sat down, Avi said, "Pinky, you've got to listen to me . . ."

"Can't it wait?" I said around a mouthful of chicken. "Tell me later."

After we finished eating dinner, we all turned our chairs to face the front of the room.

Max's magic show was about to begin!

Chapter Seven

Max wore a white shirt, a black vest, and a tall magician's top hat. "Ladies and gentlemen!" he roared. "I am about to amaze and mystify you with my feats of magic!"

"I've watched him do this trick a million times," Shira whispered in my ear.

"For my first trick, you will observe the tube I am holding in my hand." He held up a cardboard tube and waved it in front of the audience. "As you can plainly see, there is nothing inside."

The audience nodded in agreement. Then Max chanted, "Hocus pocus!" and pulled a colorful scarf from the tube.

We applauded loudly, and Max took a deep bow. "For my next trick," he said, "I will need a volunteer."

"Pinky, raise your hand so he'll pick you!" Avi insisted.

"You do it, Avi! I don't want go up there." It's not that I'm shy or anything, but standing up in front of people makes my pits get all sweaty and stinky.

Max pointed his finger at me. "Pinky Bloom, I invite you to come on up and be my assistant."

The audience chanted, "Pin*ky*, Pin*ky*, Pin*ky*, Pin*ky*," as I slowly got up from my seat and walked to the front of the room.

Max showed me a coin he had in his hand. "Pinky, will you please tell the audience what I'm holding?" he said.

"It's a quarter," I announced.

Next, Max made a fist and waved his other hand over it. "Abracadabra!" he chanted.

He opened his hand and showed the audience that the quarter had disappeared!

Suddenly, someone in the back of the social hall yelled, "The coin! It's gone!"

I looked toward the back of the room. It was Mr. Carlson, the synagogue's caretaker.

"Don't worry—Max will get it back," an audience member assured him. "It's just part of the act."

"No, the coin Mrs. Glick donated. It's been stolen!" Mr. Carlson cried.

Everyone started talking at once.

"What's going on?"

"Was there a robbery in the synagogue?"

"Did anyone see what happened?"

Mr. Newman stood up. "People, please, stay calm. We'll look into this right away. No need to panic."

I hurried back to our table. "This is terrible, Pinky!" Shira said. "My dad told me he planned to auction off that coin and use the money for a new roof for the synagogue. Now he might get in trouble for losing it. Pinky, you've got to help us find the coin!"

I'm not a magician, but magically, a new mystery had appeared. And I, Pinky Bloom, Brooklyn's greatest kid detective, was going to solve it!

Chapter Eight

The Hanukkah party ended early. After a thorough search, the coin was officially declared missing, and the police were called to investigate. Shira said that I could come by her house tomorrow for an update.

Lucy's parents arrived to take her home. "So sorry," Mr. Chang said when he heard what had happened. "But I know you can help solve the crime, Pinky. Just like you did for our restaurant."

On our way home, Avi asked, "Why would anyone take an old coin? You can't even buy good stuff like an electric scooter or a video game."

"Actually, a thief could sell that coin for lots of money and buy just about anything," Dad said.

"Doesn't the synagogue have security cameras?" Mom asked.

"They do," I answered. "And Shira told me that's what the police will look at."

Grandma Phyllis was waiting for us when we got home. "So, how was the Hanukkah party?" she asked.

Avi told her, "An old coin was stolen, and we never even got to play dreidel."

"But Mr. Carlson gave me a bunch of leftover gelt, since we didn't have time to play games," I said. I added that Shira had asked me to help solve the mystery.

"I'm going to help too!" Avi declared.

"Don't count on it," I mumbled under my breath.

Before bed, I grabbed a pencil and my detective notebook and looked through the cases I had solved.

Case #1 was when I found my cousin Rachel's retainer. Her dog had buried it in their backyard.

For Case #2, I recovered a Kiddush cup that was stolen from the Jewish Museum, and I solved the mysterious goings-on in the Lotus Blossom Kosher Chinese Restaurant owned by Lucy's parents.

I turned to a fresh page in my notebook and wrote, *CASE #3*.

WHAT: a stolen coin

WHEN: last night

WHERE: the synagogue

SUSPECTS:

I left that last entry blank. Maybe I would know more tomorrow once I found out what was on the synagogue's security footage.

Avi settled into the blow-up mattress in a corner of my room.

"You'd better not snore!" I warned him before turning out the light.

I was about to fall asleep when Avi said, "Pinky, are you awake?"

"What do you want, Avi?" I whispered.

"You know when I was hiding behind that plant in the lobby?" he said.

"Yeah. What about it?"

"I saw who took the coin!"

I bolted upright in bed. "Who took it, Avi? And you'd better not make this up."

"It was Judah Maccabee!"

Chapter Nine

Judah Maccabee was a rebel warrior who led a small army of men, women, and children. Together they restored the Temple in Jerusalem more than 2,000 years ago.

"Avi, you must be dreaming. There's no way it could have been Judah Maccabee! He isn't even alive."

"But I saw him with my own eyes. He really was there, and he took the coin. Then you came into the lobby, and he was gone."

The synagogue's security footage would tell us if

Avi was right. But I was ready to bet my new camera that the thief wasn't Judah Maccabee!

Just in case, I made a list in my head of the possible reasons why anyone would want to be Judah Maccabee:

1. They were really into Hanukkah.
2. The costume was left over from Halloween.
3. Avi was making this stuff up.

Finally, I grabbed my detective notebook and a pencil off my bedside table. Under *SUSPECTS* I wrote, *Judah Maccabee.*

In the morning, I walked into the kitchen to find Grandma Phyllis making breakfast. "Good morning, Pinky," she said. "You're up early."

I didn't tell her that Avi's snoring and my thoughts about the case had kept waking me up. "I'm meeting with Shira this morning," I said. "We're going to figure out what happened to the coin."

"Darling, you should take your brother with you. He's a very clever boy, and he can help with the investigation."

Really? Take Avi with me? No way did I want him tagging along while I was working on a case.

D. J. let out a loud growl to let me know it was

time for his breakfast. I poured dried cat food into his bowl, and he gave me a grateful "Meow."

My dad walked into the kitchen. "Pinky, I'll drive you and Avi to Shira's house on my way to work."

"Does Avi have to go?" I said. "Shira and I have important things to talk about."

Dad poured himself a cup of coffee. "Your brother is helping Max with his new magic trick. Be ready to leave in ten minutes."

On the car ride to Shira's, Dad listened to the news on the radio while Avi and I talked.

"Max is going to teach me magic tricks," Avi said excitedly. "I'm going to learn how to make things disappear."

"Speaking of disappearing things . . ." I flipped open my notebook, which I'd brought with me. "Tell me more about Judah Maccabee. What did he look like?"

"He looked *like Judah Maccabee!*" Avi insisted. "He had a helmet and a long cloak and a shield."

"But what about his face?"

"I didn't get a good look at his face because of the helmet."

"Well, did you hear him say anything?"

"Of course I did, Pinky. He was talking on his cell phone."

"Why didn't you tell me that last night?!" I shrieked.

"You didn't ask me that question."

I tried to stay calm. "Okay. What did he say?"

"I don't know."

"Avi, if you heard him talking on his phone, you must know what he said."

"Well, I don't."

"Why not?"

"Because he was speaking in Hebrew!"

I sighed. "Okay, so now I'm looking for a Judah Maccabee who has a cell phone and speaks Hebrew." This case was getting weirder and weirder!

Chapter Ten

Dad dropped us off in front of Shira's house. "Pinky, what time do you want me to pick you up?" he asked.

"Madame Olga can bring us home," I said. "She's staying with Shira and Max because the Newmans went to work."

Shira rushed out of her house. "Pinky, I'm so happy you're here!" she said. "Max is waiting for Avi in his room."

Madame Olga was in the kitchen. She wore a long, flowery skirt, and hanging from a chain around her neck was a *hamesh* hand to ward off the evil eye.

"You two must be hungry," she said. "Come eat a little something."

In between bites of carrot sticks and hummus, I asked Shira about the security video. "Could the police see who took the coin?"

"My dad said they saw someone dressed up like Judah Maccabee, but they couldn't tell who it was."

Avi likes to make things up. Like the time he told me that if you swallowed gum, it would stay in your stomach for seven years. But this time he was right!

"Pinky, there are so many questions about what happened," Shira said. "How do we find the answers?"

I turned to Madame Olga. "Did you bring your crystal ball?" I said.

"I donated it to charity, *bubeleh*. Here, I have my tablet. Brand new and works better."

Shira and I watched as she pulled out her tablet and made an internet browser appear on the screen. "What do you want to know, darling?"

"Search for Judah Maccabee costumes," I said.

Madame Olga tried that. "Hmm, lots of pictures of kids who made their own costumes," she said, swiping through images.

One year for Purim, I got dressed up as Queen Esther. I made my costume from an old bedsheet.

Then I cut out a cardboard crown and glued on fake jewels. It was fun, but the costume probably didn't look very convincing.

"Avi thought the thief really looked like Judah Maccabee," I said. "I don't think the thief was wearing a homemade costume."

"Then I'll try *Hanukkah costume stores in New York*," Madame Olga said. The results of her search popped up on the screen a second later.

"Aha!" said Madame Olga. "Okay—we go to the costume store in Borough Park. There, we'll learn who bought the Judah Maccabee costume."

Avi rushed into the kitchen. "Hey, everyone, come watch Max's new trick. He's going to make his pet tarantula disappear."

"We can't now, Avi," I said. "We're going with Madame Olga to the costume store."

"Can Max come with us? We can look for his tarantula later."

Madame Olga agreed. "We can walk to the store. It's only a few blocks away."

Avi, Shira, Max, and I put on our coats.

It was a long shot, but right now I didn't have much to go on.

Chapter Eleven

The costume store was sandwiched between a bank and a bakery on a busy street in Borough Park.

"I'm hungry," Avi said. "Can I have a donut?"

"We'll get donuts later," Madame Olga assured him. "Come look at the costumes."

Mannequins in the storefront window were dressed in pirate, superhero, and clown costumes. There was even a costume for a dog!

We walked into the store, and a clerk hurried over to us. "We're having a sale on Halloween costumes," she said. "Fifty percent off."

"Do you sell Hanukkah costumes?" I asked.

She thought for a minute. "We have a dreidel costume and a hat that's shaped like a menorah. And we had at least one Judah Maccabee. We sold one of those the other day, but I'll check in the back to see if there are more."

While we waited for her to come back, I tried on the menorah hat. "How do I look?" I asked Shira.

"Very stylish," she said, smiling. "You should wear that to services on Shabbat."

"They have a magician's cape and top hat!" Max exclaimed. "That's what I'm buying with my Hanukkah money."

Avi found a fake mustache. He held it under his nose. "This tickles," he said, laughing.

The clerk came out from the back of the store. "Sorry. I couldn't find any other Judah Maccabee costumes. I guess the one we sold the other day was our last one."

"Do you know who bought it?" Shira asked eagerly.

"We have so many customers—I can't remember them all. But I remember that he said he was buying it for a friend. Oh, and he left something behind. I didn't notice it until after he left the store."

This could be my lucky day! I held my breath as the clerk reached behind the counter and handed me a small, white paper bag. "Here it is," she said.

I reached into the bag and pulled out a gross jelly donut with teeth marks where someone had taken a bite! I was about to dump the bag in the trash when Avi yelled, "Stop, Pinky! Don't do it!"

"I wasn't going to eat it! I don't even like jelly donuts."

Then Avi said something that made perfect sense—which honestly doesn't happen too often.

"Pinky, maybe Judah Maccabee left his finger-prints on the bag."

Why hadn't I thought of that? I looked closely at the bag and spotted a single, greasy fingerprint.

"Bingo!" I exclaimed. This was a good, solid clue. "Now I just have to find out whose fingerprint this is."

"Pinky, what if it just belongs to someone in the bakery?" Shira asked.

"I can answer that," Madame Olga said. "People who make and serve ready-to-eat food have to wear throwaway gloves, so that fingerprint doesn't belong to them."

I took out my pencil and my detective notebook. Under *SUSPECTS*, I wrote, *Likes jelly donuts.*

Chapter Twelve

Dad was waiting for us when Madame Olga brought us home. "How was your visit to Shira and Max's house?" he asked.

"We went to a costume store, and they had a mustache that I wanted to buy," Avi said.

Dad laughed. "Wait a few years, and you can grow the real thing! How about you, Pinky? What did you find in the costume store?"

I told him about the Judah Maccabee costume and how Avi came up with the greasy fingerprint clue.

"Your brother is turning out to be a good detective, just like his sister," Dad said.

Avi got a big, cheesy grin on his face. "I'm going to be a secret agent *and* a detective!"

Exactly what I needed. First, he'd stolen my sunglasses. Now he was trying to steal my job!

I waited until Avi went to his room before I asked Dad if I could go to Madame Olga's tomorrow. She'd offered to teach Shira and me how to make Hanukkah candles. I didn't want Avi deciding he wanted to be a candlemaker next.

At dinnertime, we lit our family menorah, but I kept glancing over at the Glicks' menorah, which we had moved to the bookcase. Was the magical menorah going to bring us any other surprises?

Dad led us in singing the Hanukkah song "Maoz Tzur." We had just finished when the doorbell rang.

It was the super, Mr. Norman. "Hello. I'm here to see what's wrong with your lights."

Dad jumped up from the table. "I'm glad you came. They keep going on and off. I'm not sure why."

"I'll try my best to fix the problem. Could be as simple as changing a fuse."

I turned around and watched him do something to the fuse box in the kitchen. Then he walked over to the bookcase and paused to look at the menorah.

"That's Mrs. Glick's menorah," Avi told him. "She said it's magical, and it really is!"

"It must be very precious," Mr. Norman said. "Doesn't she want it back for Hanukkah?"

"She went away, and we're keeping it until she gets home," I answered.

"That's very nice of you," Mr. Norman said. "Well, I guess I'll get going. The lights should be okay now."

After Mr. Norman left, I went to my room. My detective notebook was sitting on my desk. The only name I had written down on the suspects list was Judah Maccabee.

I thought about everyone who'd been at the Hanukkah party and had access to the coin. There was Mr. Carlson, the synagogue's caretaker, and Shira's dad. Either one could have easily taken it, but neither of them had a clear motive.

I wouldn't have much time to look for new clues tomorrow, since I would be busy making candles at Madame Olga's. An art project would be fun, but I worried that I was running out of time to crack the case. Winter break was almost over, and I still hadn't solved this mystery!

Chapter Thirteen

It was almost time to leave for Madame Olga's. "I'll drive you there," Mom said.

Avi tugged on my sleeve. "Pinky, making candles is my favorite thing to do, so why can't I come with you?"

That was totally not true! Avi's idea of an art project is folding paper airplanes and shooting them across the living room.

"Nice try, Avi," I said. "But it's just going to be Shira and me."

I had just finished packing up a few things when

the lights in our apartment flickered on and off *again!*

Could someone be doing it on purpose? And why would they want the lights to go off?

Dad was in front of his computer in the living room. "I thought Mr. Norman fixed the problem," he sighed. "We'll have to call him again."

Mom dropped me off at Madame Olga's building. When I walked inside, I saw the handwritten sign posted on her apartment door: *THE PSYCHIC IS IN. PLEASE KNOCK. I MIGHT BE TAKING MY NAP.*

I knocked. The door opened, and Madame Olga ushered me inside. "Come in, Pinky," she said. "Shira is already here. We'll make candles in the kitchen. I have everything ready."

On the kitchen table was a sheet of beeswax, a knife, and a ball of string. "So first, darlings, you watch what I do, and then you'll make them yourselves," Madame Olga instructed us.

She cut a long, narrow strip from the beeswax and rolled it tightly around a length of string. "Easy," she said, holding up a candle. "Now you girls try."

"Do we have to make forty-four candles?" Shira asked.

"Only one for now," Madame Olga reassured her.

It was fun to make one candle, but I'm really okay with buying them in the store.

Shira and I helped with the cleanup. Then I told Madame Olga that we still didn't know who had stolen the coin.

Madame Olga thought for a moment. "So let me tell you something. I know a coin maven."

"What's a maven?" Shira asked.

"Someone who knows a lot about something. So, we eat lunch, I call your parents, and then we go see Jake."

Maybe it would take a maven to help me solve this mystery.

Chapter Fourteen

Shira, Madame Olga, and I walked three blocks to the train station. As we got closer, we could hear the roar of the elevated trains.

"I packed snacks for our trip to Jake's," Madame Olga said. "A little something to nosh in case you get hungry."

Madame Olga's idea of a snack was enough food to feed the entire population of Brooklyn!

Our subway car was crowded, but we were able to sit next to each other. It was only eight stops to 86th Street, and then we walked the rest of the way.

Soon, we came to a shop with a sign that said, *Jake's Antique Coins & Collectables*. Under that were the words *We Buy and Sell Rare Coins*.

We walked inside and looked around. If this was some kid's room, their mom would make them clean up and put away all their stuff.

The store was packed with pots and pans, birdcages, fish tanks, old movie posters, road signs, and New York City souvenirs. I even saw a tiny Statue of Liberty pencil sharpener like the one I got when I went on a field trip to Liberty Island.

I looked around for the coins. "Over here," Madame Olga said, pointing to a short glass cabinet that ran along one wall.

A man came over to us. "Hello! I'm Jake," he said. "Are you looking for something in particular?"

"Do you have any old coins from Israel?" I asked.

"You've come to the right place, young lady. Let me show you what I have."

Jake reached into the glass case and took out a tray of coins. "These shekels are from Israel," he said. "In ancient times, they were a unit of weight. Later, they were used as coinage to buy things."

"Why do they have pictures of trees and plants instead of pictures of presidents?" Shira asked.

"Jews obeyed the Second Commandment, and coins weren't allowed to have graven images," Jake explained. "They couldn't use pictures of people, who might be seen as more important than God."

I pulled out my camera and showed Jake the photo of Mrs. Glick's coin. "Can you tell us anything about this one?" I asked.

He looked closely at the photo. "If I had to guess, I'd say it might be a shekel from the time of the Jewish revolt against Rome, which was around 66–70 in the Common Era."

"How much money is it worth?" I asked.

"A Judean coin from that time recently sold at auction for a million dollars."

Madame Olga gasped. "So much money! The synagogue would be able help so many people."

"Not so fast," Jake said. "Most coins that look like this are counterfeit—fake. That means they're worthless."

"What if they have a certificate of authenticity that says they're real?" I asked.

"Anyone could make something like that," he said. "Fake coins are a big business. Lots of people get fooled into paying a lot of money for them."

Could Mrs. Glick's coin be fake? This mystery was like a roller coaster. It had so many twists and turns that I was holding on tight, hoping I wouldn't fall off!

Chapter Fifteen

Lucy was waiting for me when I got home. "Pinky, what have you learned about the missing coin?" she asked.

"Madame Olga's friend Jake thinks it could be a fake," I explained. "He told us the way counterfeit coins are made."

"How do they do it?" Lucy wanted to know.

"According to Jake, the counterfeiters press the real coin into two pieces of clay to make an imprint of each side. Then they seal the clay imprints together with liquid rubber to make a mold. After the rubber hardens, they pour melted metal into the gap in the mold where the coin used to be. When *that* hardens, they have a replica of the coin."

"Wow!" said Lucy. "That sounds like a lot of work. But I guess it's worth it if they can sell the fake coins for a ton of money."

"Here's the strange thing, though," I said. "Counterfeiters need a *real* coin to make the fake copies. And *real* ancient Israeli coins are really rare."

"So if the donated coin was fake, where's the real coin that the counterfeiters used to make it?" asked Lucy, catching my drift. "And how did they get ahold of such a rare coin in the first place?"

I still didn't have a lot of answers, so I sat down at Dad's computer and typed in a question.

"Lucy, it says here that all ancient artifacts discovered on Israeli soil are the property of the state. That means people aren't supposed to take them out of Israel."

"So it would be *extra* hard for someone to get a coin like that," said Lucy.

"Right." I frowned. "And that means Buzzy Glick wasn't supposed to bring the coin here. Or the magical menorah!"

Before I could think about this more, Avi marched into the living room. "I'm helping with your case, Pinky," he announced. "Do you want to hear what I'm going to do?"

"Not really, Avi. But go ahead anyway. Just make it fast."

"I'm dusting for fingerprints," he said, holding up the small brush from his spy kit. In his other hand, he held the donut bag we'd gotten at the costume store. "Maybe I'll find a match with the thief's print."

I rolled my eyes. "Avi, you're only going to find *our* fingerprints, because we live here!"

"Uh-uh, Pinky. Just wait."

Lucy and I watched as Avi dusted the living room desk. "No match here," he mumbled. "Only Dad's fingerprints."

Then he moved on to the windowsill. "Just Mom's prints. I'll try the bookcase next."

"Avi, you and I have touched that bookcase a million times," I said. "And so have Mom, Dad, and Grandma Phyllis. You're never going to find a match."

"You're wrong, Pinky! Look at this!" he shouted.

I raced over to see what he had found. A fingerprint on the bookcase matched the one on the donut bag!

"See? They're the same," Avi said gleefully. "That means Judah Maccabee was right here in our apartment."

It took a minute for this to sink in. And when I realized what it meant, I got goose bumps all over!

Chapter Sixteen

After Lucy had to leave, I grabbed my notebook. Under *SUSPECTS*, I crossed out *Judah Maccabee* and wrote *Mr. Norman*.

He'd been here in our apartment fixing the lights. And I'd seen him by the bookcase, staring at the magical menorah!

It was time to do some snooping. Mom was on her cell phone, and Dad was at work. I wrote them a note that said I was going to Madame Olga's and would be back soon.

"Can I come too, Pinky?" Avi pleaded.

"No, you may not. And that's final!"

"I'll make you a deal, Pinky. I'll give you back your sunglasses if you take me with you."

I really wanted those sunglasses back, so I agreed that he could come along.

Before we left, Avi stuffed his night goggles, a flashlight, and a cookie into his backpack.

"Do you really need all that stuff?" I said. "We're only going to Madame Olga's. It's a block away."

"Secret agents always have to be prepared," Avi said as we headed out the door.

Luckily, Madame Olga was at home. "A visit from two of my favorite children!" she gushed. "What can I help you with?"

I told her how the greasy fingerprint matched Mr. Norman's. "We think he was the one who wore the Judah Maccabee costume and stole the coin."

"*Oy vey*," she said, shaking her head. "If that's true, this super could be in big trouble."

"Madame Olga, what do we do now?" I asked.

"We look for the evidence, Pinky. I think he has a workshop, no? Let's see what we can find in there."

Madame Olga, Avi, and I walked back to my building and took the elevator down to the basement.

The door to Mr. Norman's workshop was wide open. And he was nowhere in sight!

"Take a quick look around, and don't touch anything," Madame Olga said.

Mr. Norman had tons of stuff in his workshop. There were hammers, screwdrivers, cans of paint, brushes, snow shovels, work boots, and a floor polisher.

I wasn't sure what exactly we were looking for. Then Avi yelled, "Come quick! Look what I found!"

Hanging on the back of the workshop door was the Judah Maccabee costume!

"That must be the costume Mr. Norman wore the night of the Hanukkah party!" I cried.

There was a long red cloak, a white shirt, a black cloth belt, and a pair of black pants. A plastic shield and helmet hung on a nearby hook.

I looked at the label inside the shirt collar. It said the costume was a size medium.

My dad wears a size large. Mr. Norman is much bigger and taller than he is, and that made me wonder about the costume.

Was Mr. Norman pretending to be Judah Maccabee—or was it someone else?

Chapter Seventeen

One other thing caught my eye in Mr. Norman's workshop. It was a closet door with signs that said *PRIVATE PROPERTY! DANGER! DO NOT ENTER!*

Madame Olga had said not to touch anything, but I was curious about what was behind that door.

I put my hand on the knob. The door creaked open, and I saw a hallway! But where did it lead?

There was only one way to find out. "You go first," I told Avi. "We'll be right behind you."

Avi didn't budge. "What's it worth, Pinky?" he said.

I thought for a moment. "Okay—you know the leftover gelt Mr. Carlson gave me when we left the Hanukkah party? You can have it."

So Avi took the lead, and Madame Olga and I followed in single file.

At the end of the hallway, we came to another room that was much smaller than the workshop.

"This Mr. Norman has a secret," Madame Olga said, looking around. "So what was he doing in here?"

The room was no bigger than a closet. Stacked on shelves were bags of clay, bars of metal, an electric hot pot, and a carton of liquid rubber. I took pictures of everything in case it could be important evidence.

Avi looked around. "Maybe he was making a sword for his Judah Maccabee costume," he said.

Madame Olga said the hot pot might be used to make new apartment keys. "First, you melt metal, and then you pour it into a mold," she said.

That reminded me of what Jake had told us when we were in his store.

I was about to say what I was thinking when the lights in Mr. Norman's secret closet went out!

"Stay where you are," Madame Olga cautioned us. "I'll look for a light switch. It's got to be around here somewhere."

"I've got my night googles and a flashlight!" Avi said. "We don't need to turn on the lights."

Maybe it wasn't so bad having a secret agent for a brother!

Avi focused the flashlight's beam on the hallway. Slowly and carefully, we made our way back to the workshop, where the lights were still working.

I had a pretty good idea of what was going on, but I had to come up with a way to prove it!

Chapter Eighteen

"There you are," Mom said when Madame Olga brought Avi and me back to our apartment. "We were starting to get worried."

"Now that you're here, we can have a nice, quiet dinner," Dad said.

"I have to wash my hands first," I said.

A minute later, I rushed out of the bathroom and shouted, "The toilet's overflowing! Quick—someone call Mr. Norman!"

My plan was in place. I crossed my fingers and hoped it was going to work!

Mom made the call. Mr. Norman showed up and headed to the bathroom. A few minutes later, he came out to the living room. "You can use the toilet now," he said. "One of your kids stuffed it up with toilet paper!"

Grandma Phyllis handed him a plate. "Please, stay and have something to eat," she said.

It was time for my big reveal. I walked to the front of the room and said, "I, Pinky Bloom, Brooklyn's greatest kid detective, will now tell you what happened to Mrs. Glick's coin."

Mr. Norman jumped up from his seat. "I really have to go," he said. "Apartment 214's got a leaky faucet."

Avi pointed a finger at him. "You were the one who dressed up like Judah Maccabee!" he shouted.

"Not true, young man. You must be mistaken. It wasn't me."

I looked over at Avi. "He's right," I said. "It was someone else who wore the costume."

"But we found it in his workshop! And I saw Judah Maccabee take the coin at the Hanukkah party!"

"I also thought it was Mr. Norman at first," I said.

"Then I realized he couldn't have worn the costume, because it didn't fit him!"

Mr. Norman patted his belly. "Comes from eating too many donuts," he said.

"But Mr. Norman isn't innocent," I went on. "He was working with Judah Maccabee. And he's got a secret room in his workshop where he makes counterfeit coins!" I held up my camera. "I have pictures to prove it."

Everyone in the room gasped.

Mr. Norman pulled out a tissue and wiped his sweaty face. "Okay, okay! But it wasn't my idea."

"That's against the law!" Dad shouted.

The doorbell rang. Mom answered it, and in walked Buzzy Glick! "I've come to collect my menorah," he said. "But I see you have company, so I'll come back another time."

"Please join us, Mr. Glick," I said. "And tell us why you stole the coin!"

Buzzy looked around at all of us. After a moment, he sighed. "The coin was fake," he admitted. "My mom didn't know that when she donated it to the synagogue."

"Why would you steal a worthless coin?" Dad asked.

It was my turn again. "Because he didn't want anyone to find out about the counterfeiting operation that he and Mr. Norman set up in the basement of our building!"

"Look, I don't want any trouble," Buzzy said. "I'm taking my menorah, and I'm out of here."

He ran over to the bookcase and grabbed the menorah. But as he turned around, he startled D. J., who'd been sitting on the floor next to the bookcase. Buzzy tripped over the cat, and the menorah slipped out of his hand.

The menorah fell on the floor, and an Israeli shekel dropped out of a candleholder.

I bent down and picked it up. "Is this a fake, Mr. Glick? Or is it the real thing?"

"It's real," he said. "I found it a long time before the laws changed, so I was allowed to take it out of Israel."

"Having the coin might be legal," Dad said. "But it's still not okay to use it to make fakes!"

"I've had enough," Mr. Norman said, edging his way toward the door. "Let's go, Buzzy!"

Grandma Phyllis blocked the door. "Not so fast," she said. "The only place you two will be going is jail!"

Chapter Nineteen

Lucy, Madame Olga, and the Newmans joined us for the last night of Hanukkah.

Shira caught me up on the case. "The police charged Buzzy Glick and Mr. Norman with counterfeiting," she reported.

"Will they go to jail?" Avi asked.

"Probably not," Mr. Newman said. "But they'll have to pay back all the people who bought their fake coins." Then he turned to me. "Pinky, I'd like to thank you for all your help with this."

"How did you know the real coin was hidden

in the magical menorah?" Shira asked me.

"I didn't!" I said. "The coin fit perfectly in the candleholder, and since it was silver, it blended in. We never noticed it."

"But why was it in the menorah?" Lucy asked.

"That's where Buzzy Glick hid it for safekeeping," I said. "He didn't know that his mom would leave the menorah with us. He found out when he talked to Mrs. Glick on the phone. Then Mr. Norman turned our lights on and off so he would have an excuse to come to our apartment. He wanted to get the real coin from the menorah while we were distracted."

"So the menorah isn't magic?" said Avi, sounding disappointed.

"I don't think so," I said. "Except . . . the candles all went out at once on the first night of Hanukkah."

"Oh, that?" said Grandma Phyllis. "I blew them out, darling. The cat was getting a little too interested in the open flames!"

We all laughed, except for D. J., who looked offended.

"Let's light the magical menorah tonight!" Avi said. "Mrs. Glick is still away, and she won't mind."

"We can use the candle Pinky made," Madame Olga suggested.

Everyone gathered around the magical menorah. All the candles burned brightly, even the one I made!

After we said the prayer, Avi reminded me about the bag of chocolate gelt I'd promised him. "I'll share it with everybody," he said. Sometimes, even the world's most annoying little brother isn't so bad.

I got the bag from my room and dumped the gelt on the dining room table. Mixed in with the chocolate was the fake coin that Buzzy Glick stole!

"Buzzy Glick knew that the coin was worthless," I said. "He must've just wanted to get rid of it. So he dropped it into the pile of gelt that Mr. Carlson scooped up and gave to me!"

Shira gave me a big hug. "Pinky, you really are Brooklyn's greatest detective!" she said.

Her dad said that he was already planning next year's Hanukkah party. "Avi and Max will perform magic tricks—but they won't be allowed to make a coin disappear!"

After everyone went home, I took out my notebook. Next to *CASE #3*, I wrote, *SOLVED!*

Hanukkah was officially over, and I would be back at school tomorrow.

It would be a nice change from being a detective— unless another mystery appeared, just like magic!

About the Author

Judy Press studied fine arts at Syracuse University and earned a masters in art education from the University of Pittsburgh. She is the creator of many award-winning children's art activity books and early reader chapter books. A grandmother to ten, she lives in Pittsburgh.

About the Illustrator

Erica-Jane Waters has been writing and illustrating children's books for more than twenty years and uses a mixture of traditional techniques and digital work to create her art. Erica-Jane lives in Northamptonshire in England with her family.